Elephant Small
is lost

by **Sally Grindley**

illustrated by **Andy Ellis**

little ORCHARD

Elephant Small was lost.
  "Where are you, Elephant
Small?" sobbed Elephant Mum.
  But there was no reply.

Jolly Dog came bounding to the rescue. "Don't worry, Elephant Mum, I'll soon sniff him out!" he said.

And he bounced off round the room.

Jolly Dog sniffed through
Dumpy Truck's bricks.
SNIFF SNIFF – OUCH!

BONK!

But Elephant Small wasn't there.

Jolly Dog sniffed behind Jack-in-the-Box.
SNIFF SNIFF – OOOH!

BOING!

But Elephant Small wasn't there.

Jolly Dog sniffed through Big Red
Tractor's straw.
SNIFF SNIFF – AATCHOO!

But Elephant Small wasn't there either.

"Where can he be?" sobbed Elephant Mum.

"Where can he be?" said the other toys.

Then they heard a little voice.
"I want my mummy!" it said.
Jolly Dog gave one enormous
sniff ... S N I F F !

And he bounced over to the chest of drawers.

It was Elephant Small.
"There you are!" cried Elephant Mum
"Mummy!" cried Elephant Small.
"I got stuck!"